Pē-Pie-Pō

The Prairie Dog
Discovers a Forest

By Josie Hudson
Illustrated by Larry Love

Printed in the United States of America

First Printing, 2014

ISBN 978-0-692-20289-0

Fish's Mouth Enterprises, LLC

PO Box 780

Pampa, TX 79066

First Edition

Pē-Pie-Pō was a prairie dog who lived in a burrow with his mama, his daddy, and his baby sister, Piper. Pē-Pie-Pō was proud of his home. Daddy had dug down deep into the clay loam prairie dirt…

…down past the earthworms…dowr past the buffalo grass roots…and even pas the occasional ground squirrel tunnel. Pē-Pie-Pō thought it to be the biggest, best burrow ever

Then Mama added her touch...making the burrow nice and cozy. She had made a table using yucca stalks as the legs and then wove the table top from yucca leaves. She always had some tasty treat sitting out, ready to be eaten. Sometimes there were delicious roots, sometimes grasshoppers, sometimes she even had special treats like cactus berries...yum, yum, yum!

Pē-Pie-Pō was proudest of one special place in the burrow, his cozy wozy bed. Mama had made it especially for him, just the right size and just the right snuggly wuggly soft…just perfect. Made of the tall, lanky prairie grass that grew in abundance just above, it was the absolute best bed ever!!

Now as much as **Pē-Pie-Pō** loved his family's burrow, he loved exploring the prairie above him even more. Each morning he would awake with new, adventurous ideas bursting in his head. Today was one such day…

...a BEAUTIFUL spring day! Eating breakfast at the yucca table with his family, he could hear the birds twittering joyfully above him as they welcomed this new day as well.

Pē-Pie-Pō stuck his head out of the burrow, taking a big whiff of the lovely spring air. He caught the scent of newly blooming wildflowers and the wet earthy smell of the ground, moist with the morning dew. But one thing did seem a little odd, although Pē-Pie-Pō was having trouble putting his paw on it… something was missing…

As he crawled all the way out of the tunnel, it hit him…the wind! The wind was calm today, a very unusual happening on the prairie. It was common for the wind here to blow from morning till night; and many times all through the night as well.

Well, thought Pē-Pie-Pō, this is going to be an unusually WONDERFUL day of exploring!

Piper joined Pē-Pie-Pō, and together they spent the morning exploring the prairie dog town…

…meeting new friends and visiting with old. Soon dinner had come and gone, and Piper had to go down for her afternoon nap.

Pē-Pie-Pō ventured out of his burrow once more with the northern horizon catching his gaze. He had always been curious about that place. In every other direction around him, as far as his eye could see, there were flat plains filled with grass, yucca, and wildflowers. But a little way to the north, the terrain changed…

…and the prairie started to dip a bit. He wasn't quite sure, but he thought he could almost see the top of a tree.

Now Pē-Pie-Pō had never really seen a tree before, not up close anyway. So, he decided that today was the day he would change that. He gauged the distance to that tree and thought that he would most definitely be able to make it there, admire the tree, and make it back home before supper

So off he went… at quite a quick pace! Although he was traveling fast for a small prairie dog, he wasn't making as good of time as he had hoped. Pē-Pie-Pō ended up having to stop quite a lot to rest. However, the thrill of getting to see and explore a tree soon had him back on his paws, nose to the north.

Now he was almost upon it, and what an amazing thing it was! He had never seen anything as tall and majestic as this lone cottonwood tree. Why, the only thing he had ever seen taller than prairie grass was the occasional yucca, and now they seem like mere ants compared to this tree.

As Pē-Pie-Pō explored this new amazement, many more such grand cottonwood trees caught his eye. They were nestled below him by a dry creek bed.

Now Pē-Pie-Pō was pretty confident that he would be able to climb down the jagged cliff that separated him from the other trees. After all, he was an expert in climbing down into his burrow. How much harder could this be?

But, when he was a few feet from the top, he realized that it was a little different than climbing down a tunnel.

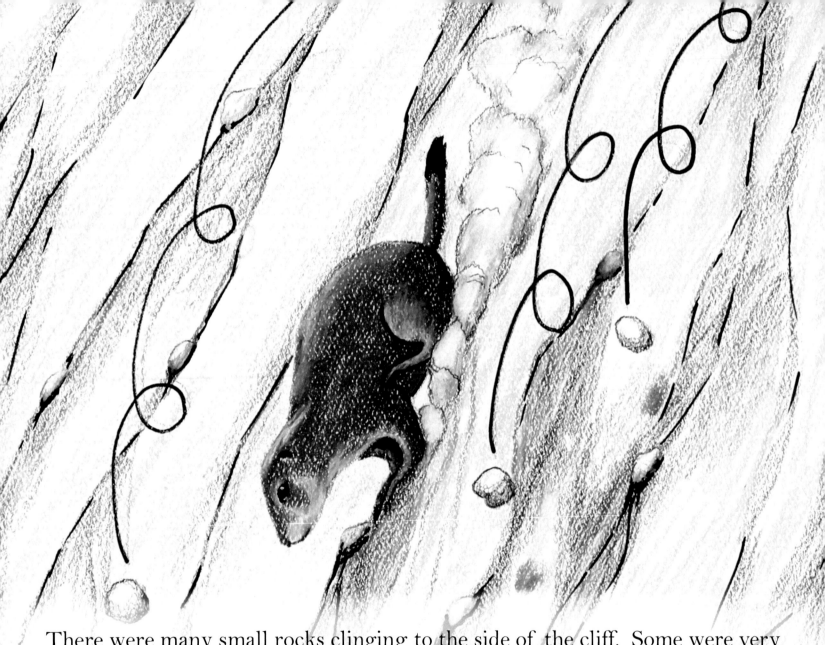

There were many small rocks clinging to the side of the cliff. Some were very stable and would easily hold his weight, but he found others to be loose and give way as soon as his paw hit them. However, after a bit he was safely at the bottom, viewing even more majestic trees.

Although there were only about eight giant
cottonwood trees strewn about the creek bed,
to Pē-Pie-Pō it seemed as if he'd found a forest.

A forest within a prairie, a pretty impressive feat if he did say so himself. Pē-Pie-Pō smiled. He was sure he would go down in the history books as the first prairie dog in his town to have found a forest.

He wondered what other unknown treasures were down here, just waiting to be discovered. Pē-Pie-Pō looked at the sun and, judging by it's position in the sky, decided he had a little more time to explore before heading home.

Pē-Pie-Pō climbed over large rocks, exploring each as he went. He dodged yuccas and cacti, going up and down ravine after ravine. Even the dry creek bed was fun to explore.

Soon, however, Pē-Pie-Pō realized that the temperature had dropped a bit, and looking up, he saw that the sun was fast approaching the horizon. It would be dark soon!! And where was he? Pē-Pie-Pō thought he knew…

…but as he looked around, he realized all the trees looked the same, and there were many tall, jagged cliffs rising above him on all sides.

He was lost….Miserably lost!! He felt like hunkering down beside the nearest yucca and falling asleep with the hope that when he awoke, he would be safe and sound in his cozy bed at home.

But Pē-Pie-Pō knew the consequences of
falling asleep out in the open prairie.
Coyotes and other predators would soon
be roaming this area for a meal. He must
find his way home soon, before nightfall.

Just then, the prairie wind began to blow. Slow at first…soon stronger and stronger. And with it came familiar scents of prairie dogs, his family and friends, and the wildflowers that bloom near his burrow, blown down from his prairie dog town…

…all the way over the prairie and down the jagged cliff, right into his nose! He bravely faced into the wind, now knowing the direction he must go, the direction that would lead him safely home.

Pē-Pie-Pō pressed on fearlessly! Up and over the rocks, up and down the ravines, around yucca and cacti, and finally all the way back up the jagged cliff. He was close to home now, so close that he could hear the chirping of his father and mother calling him for supper.

Now safely at home, tummy full, Pē-Pie-Pō's
mind ran wild with the afternoon's adventure.
He contemplated telling his parents about the
amazing prairie forest he had discovered, but knowing
that Mama would get all flustered and fretful and that Daddy
would more than likely give him a scolding, he decided he had
better keep the adventure to himself for the time being.

Pē-Pie-Pō had learned a valuable lesson that day. Going on a grand exploration all by oneself is not always the greatest idea! This adventure had shown him the seriousness and responsibility an explorer must bear. His adventure could have ended in a catastrophe!!! Thankfully it had not, but he would be much wiser the next time he went to discover the unknown. Not only would Pē-Pie-Pō be much more aware of his surroundings, he would also seek out a companion to go on the next adventure with him, and he would make sure that his parents knew of his plans.

Pē-Pie-Pō had also found a great new friend, the prairie wind. He would never again take it for granted. He now loved to face into it and feel its strong fingers blowing through his fur from the tip of his nose all the way down to the end of his black-tipped tail. Nor would he ever underestimate his sense of smell and the powerful gift that it was. The gift to not only savor and enjoy the beautiful scents that spring held, but also the gift of direction that got him back home, safe and sound.

Parent's Guide

Possible discussion topics related to Pē-Pie-Pō's adventure:

1. How might Pē-Pie-Pō's adventure have gone differently had he:

    A. Asked his parents' permission before exploring?

    B. Not gone exploring alone?

    C. Been more aware of the time and surroundings?

2. Pē-Pie-Pō's sense of smell enabled him to find his way home safely.

    A. What natural gifts, talents, abilities, and/or instincts does your child possess?

    B. Is your child aware that he/she possesses these gifts?

    C. How might you help hone and encourage these gifts in your child?